Three Little Kittens

Story by:
Michelle Baron

Illustrated by:

Theresa Mazurek	Rivka
Douglas McCarthy	Fay Whitemountain
Allyn Conley-Gorniak	Su-Zan Lewis
Lorann Downer	Lisa Souza

This Book Belongs To:

Jennifer

Use this symbol to match book and cassette.

Now that we're all together again,
I'd like to tell you a nursery rhyme.
This nursery rhyme is called "The Three
Little Kittens." Then you'll find out how
Hector meets the kittens and helps them
solve their problems.

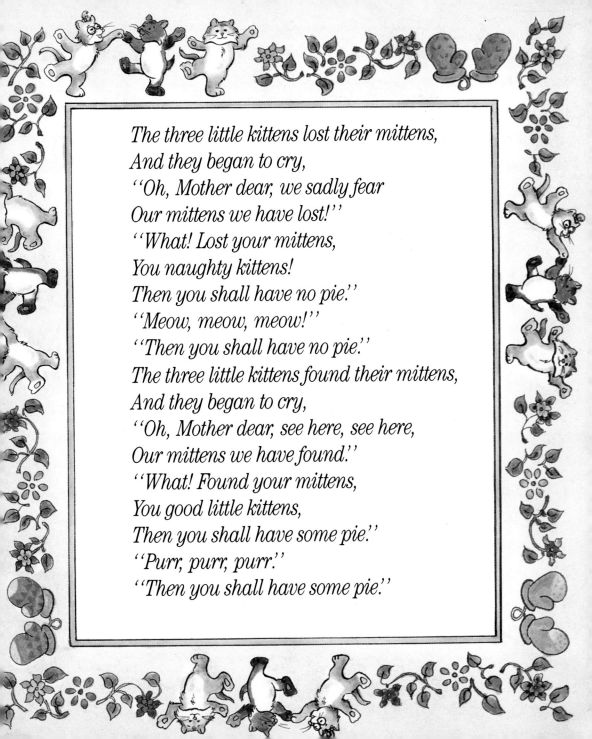

The three little kittens lost their mittens,
And they began to cry,
"Oh, Mother dear, we sadly fear
Our mittens we have lost!"
"What! Lost your mittens,
You naughty kittens!
Then you shall have no pie."
"Meow, meow, meow!"
"Then you shall have no pie."
The three little kittens found their mittens,
And they began to cry,
"Oh, Mother dear, see here, see here,
Our mittens we have found."
"What! Found your mittens,
You good little kittens,
Then you shall have some pie."
"Purr, purr, purr."
"Then you shall have some pie."

Hector wanted to know where the Three Little Kittens lost their mittens, and he wanted to know how they found them. So Hector began to look for the kittens.

Hector looked all around–under a bush, behind a rock, and inside a hollow log. But he couldn't find them.

So Hector went to sit under a tree to think about where the kittens could be.

Suddenly, a tree limb broke. The Three Little Kittens fell out of the tree and landed right in front of him!

Hector was surprised. He very politely introduced himself. The kittens introduced themselves to Hector.

Their names were Puddin', Patch and Scratch, and they were in a hurry to find their mittens.

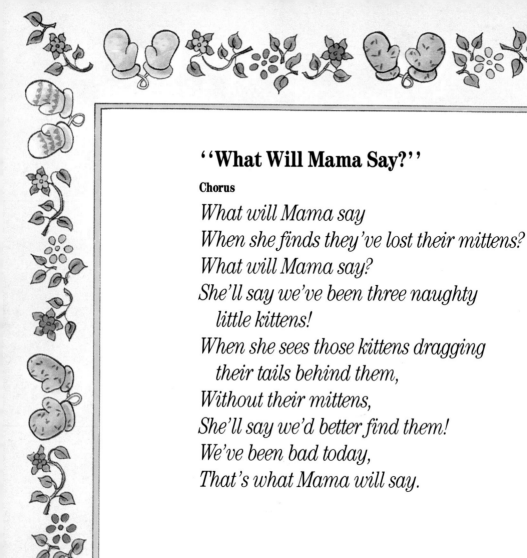

"What Will Mama Say?"

Chorus

What will Mama say
When she finds they've lost their mittens?
What will Mama say?
She'll say we've been three naughty
little kittens!
When she sees those kittens dragging
their tails behind them,
Without their mittens,
She'll say we'd better find them!
We've been bad today,
That's what Mama will say.

Mommy Goose just told me,
Remember where you were,
There's a simple way to find the things
    you lose.
Just try to think of what you did today.
But I'm not sure.
Come on, let's look for some clues.

I don't think their mother will be very
    mad at them,
Mother cats know what their kittens do.
If they promise not to lose their little
    mittens again,
Their mother will forgive them, too.

Repeat Chorus

Hector wanted to help the kittens find their mittens. He tried to tell them about thinking through their day. But the kittens wouldn't listen.

Instead, they wanted to pretend to be detectives!

The kittens were disappointed to find that playing detective hadn't helped them find their mittens.

The kittens had another idea. They would use magic to solve their problem.

But none of their magic worked.

It takes more than magic to find the things we lose, doesn't it?

The kittens were worried, so they finally listened to Hector. You know what he wanted to tell them, don't you, dear?

When you lose something, you should just stop and think it through.

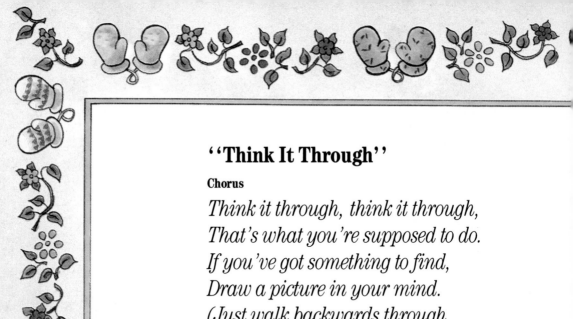

"Think It Through"

Chorus

Think it through, think it through,
That's what you're supposed to do.
If you've got something to find,
Draw a picture in your mind.
(Just walk backwards through
*   your mind.)*
Think it through from the start,
You'll remember every part.
And it all will come back to you
When you think it through.

Start with this morning and go step
  by step.
Okay, let's see. I got up out of bed.
Then I forget.
Okay, now think it through,
It was a beautiful day.
Oh yeah, we put our mittens on,
And went out to play!

Repeat Chorus

Thinking it through is sure to remind you
Of what you've done and where you've
  been today.
If you want to find what you left
  behind you,
Thinking it through is the easiest way.

Repeat Chorus

So they thought and thought and realized that they were climbing trees all day.

It's not easy for kittens to climb trees with mittens on.

The kittens remembered that they started climbing at the big oak tree, and they knew that their mittens must be there. So Hector and the kittens ran toward the oak tree as fast as they could.

When they got there, they saw
something unusual hanging right
in front of them.

It was a blanket–a quilt to be exact.
And into the quilt were sewn all sorts
of things–socks, hats, shirts, and even...
the Three Little Kittens' mittens.

A very nice mother possum was hanging upside down from the oak tree. She was making a patchwork quilt for her children, and she sewed whatever she found into the quilt! The quilt looked very unusual indeed!

Do you suppose that something you have lost may be in Mrs. Possum's quilt?

Well, Mrs. Possum gave the kittens their mittens and they were very happy. They thanked Hector for helping them "think it through."

Then the new friends said goodbye. The Three Little Kittens hurried home to show their mother that they had found their mittens…

…and to eat some pie…

…and Hector came back to tell me all about his very special day.